DAYDREAMS
and
JELLYBEANS

Alex Wharton　　　Katy Riddell

First published in 2021
by Firefly Press
25 Gabalfa Road, Llandaff North, Cardiff, CF14 2JJ
www.fireflypress.co.uk

A CIP catalogue record of this book is available
from the British Library.

ISBN 978-1-913102-43-2
ebook ISBN 978-1-913102-44-9

1 3 5 7 9 8 6 4 2

This book has been published with the support of
the Books Council of Wales.

Typeset by Hazel Guppy.
Printed by CPI Group UK.

DAYDREAMS
and
JELLYBEANS

Alex Wharton   Katy Riddell

Firefly

For Rebecca, Leo and Jermaine.
With all of my love, always. Xxx

CONTENTS

Foreword
by Philip Gross

Where is a poem most alive – most its living, breathing, dancing, thoughtful, quirky self? One answer is: when the poet is right there, speaking it. I can't imagine anyone reading this collection not wanting to meet Alex Wharton, and so you should, when you have a chance. But these poems are in your hand now, and they're packed full of Alex's voice and energy – the warmth, the moments of reflection, the sudden skitters of fun and wordplay, dropping almost to a whisper at the sight of something wonderful and strange... That's not just a poetic style; it's a personality.

These poems do what all good poems do. They get inside you. The way the words play on the page, the rhythms of the lines, you start to hear them. I'll bet you can't read through this book without your lips moving, trying out how it would sound to say them out loud. Go on. Do.

When a poet's in the room, they'll put you in the right mood for the poems, with a twinkle in their eye or thoughtful look. They'll drop a hint about the background. In this book that is happening too – in Katy Riddell's deft, delightful illustrations. The pictures, like the poems, trigger the imagination. They invite you to join in.

So, step inside and bring all of yourself with you. You'll find poems to match all kinds of feelings – when you want to hoot out loud with laughter, when you've had it up to there with your brother or sister, or when you want to be very quiet and just notice everything – poems, too, that start you wondering what it's like to be not you at all but something other, say, a football, or a waterfall. Now, that's what I mean by alive.

Night Music

I saw sounds at night,
altering the shapes of trees,

tickling shadows,
dancing on an owl's tongue,

I saw sounds skipping
from door to door,

rattling the letterbox,
slipping into dreams,

I saw a gentle drumbeat
chase a prancing fox,

amongst a tiny applause
of closing flowers.

The Paint Job

Nobody sees him
and nobody knows,
the man who paints
the lines on the roads.

My road was bare,
not a single line there,
but one day I woke up,
and they were everywhere!

White dashed lines,
struck sweet through the middle,
perfectly straight,
without a drip or squiggle!

He keeps swimming pools
of paint, gleaming white!
To fill his tins and head off
in the dead of night!

With a steady brush,
and a simple code,
PAINT STRAIGHT WHITE
LINES ON EVERY ROAD!

Snail

Just
passing through
On a Sunday afternoon   //
  As *s   l   o   w*   oo
    as I move, is   h • s
      as *s   l   o   w* as I c   e

Jellybean

There's a Jellybean
stranded at the top of the stairs,
its blue beany body
is covered in hairs.

It's *Bean* there for days
just gathering dust,
and people walk by
with a look of disgust!

So I pick the bean up,
and walk to the bin,
but I change my mind
before I throw it in.

You see, the bin was full,
and I do hate to waste,
so I chewed the bean up,
and what a wonderful taste!

Dear Brother

When you sleep:

Did you know that your mouth
unlocks itself and hangs wide

open like the entrance of a lonely
cave? It swallows the entire bedroom

only to throw it back out again on the next
breath. It's a space-like black hole

with waterfalls of dribble that
slide down your cheeks and

form warm dribbly pools on your pillow.
There's usually some snot too –

slowly lodging and clogging up
the background mechanics of your

nostrils. And when you breathe in it sounds
like a crisp packet jammed in the nozzle

of a hoover! Anyway, it's the kind of
sound that clings to every particle

of air. There's no escaping it, which is why
your new bedroom … is in the shed

at the very bottom of the garden.
(Not our garden either) … Goodnight.

Mrs Patterson

Mrs Patterson has one thousand clocks,
and she loves them all,
they are busy on the shelves
and they are busy on the walls,

some were gifts over the years
from family now passed away,
Mrs Patterson is 90 today!

And they tick and they tock,
they chirp and they chime,
keeping rhythm, keeping time.

But just like people,
worn out by the day,
when night sweeps in,
they have less to say,

the second hand still ticks,
but in a gentler way,
and the bells still chime,
but from far away,

like an echo of a whisper
or the sound of snow,
hard to explain,
(but I think you know):

Why ring loud if there's no one around?
To sleep at night we shelter sound.

And when morning returns,
so do the chimes,
and the ticks and tocks,
the measurements of time,

they slip through the cat flap,
and shake the night off,
then wake Mrs Patterson,
with eight bells of the clock.

Kingfisher

I saw you,
zipping through threads
of shallow summer air,
blue into green.
Where do you rest?
Where is your fishbone nest?

I saw you again in
your sunbeam vest,
orange into blue,
your laser-tight-flight
splits time in two.

I saw your whistle,
holding onto your wings.
When you arrow-into-water,
the ripples sing.

And branches stretch-the-river,
for one tickle of your flame,
for a sprinkle of stardust,
you're worth the risk, *they say*.

Spiders

Of course, spiders play an important role in the
  ecosystem, imagine how many flies there would be
  without spiders eating them for their tea.
  I appreciate that, I do,
But I can't help but wish they were less,
you know, terrifying!
Those eight-legged eerie-eyed, sometimes hairy,
  always shady
friends of ours. They will hide in your shoes! So always
check before slipping
in that innocent foot. They are terrific on their tiptoes,
  daintily sneaking
amongst shadows. Notice how they scale up a wall and
  over the ceiling like
an orbiting moon. Watch them swing on a single
  thread of silver web and always
land correct like a clever-clog-cat. Some have
  ludicrously long legs and they walk
as if slowly lunging over puddles in the pavement,
Others have tiny legs that run rapidly like someone
  desperate to use the loo. And if you ever spot one
  scurrying across your living room floor, then you
  will probably witness its extraordinary acting
  abilities.
(All courtesy of the Young Spiders Secret Society)*

Some will leap like accomplished gymnasts, hoping
    that you too, will leap – in a
freaky-fright and therefore lose sight of the
crafty imposter.
Or you may see the less common 'Spider ball' tactic
    used, where the spider
(when seen) scrunches itself into a miniature ball and
    rolls with spider
speed to the nearest uncatchable space. But most
    commonly they will
adopt the 'Statue stance' with their long legs and
    multiple eyes
frozen in position – But beware!
It is **vital** that you keep a keen eye on the slippery
    figure. Do. Not. Blink!
Because if you do, the spider is sure to have vanished.
And when you see it next,
It will be

TEn TIMES BIGGER!!!

*– Young Spiders Secret Society or Y.S.S.S for
short - is a special agency that trains spiders
in the art of temporary disappearance,
drama, rapid growth and general creepiness.*

Waterfall

You are all water,
and all water is you,
this time, you search
for a pool to fall into.
a journey into water
is a journey home.
wandering, folding,
bursting and stretching
like wet flames,
turn inside and over,
roll into new water,
and gather every sound,
carry them off the
edge of ground.
every stone smoothed
and riverbed tickled.
each dip and twist
of bird and fish.
you fall again,
together
again,

whisper
burble
thunder
hiss.

Mr Madewrong

They built me without instructions,
couldn't be bothered to read them
apparently there's no need,
but I disagree.

My head is stuck on backwards,
I have two left feet,
my mouth is upside down,
do I sound complete?

My arms are always swinging,
they forgot to give me knees,
my hips are always wiggling,
dodgy wiring, I believe.

But I'm a good toy,
we all have complications,
I just want you to know,
there's nothing wrong with instructions!

Star Control

The stars that glisten
for you at night,
are selected by star control,

A celestial team that
blend shade and light,
for magic to unfold,

They sail through space,
a magnificent sight,
on an upside-down rainbow,

And they look similar to us,
but with galaxies for eyes,
and skin that is glittered with gold.

So when you're lying in bed,
and stars are pulsing above,
like diamonds drifting on shadows,

Let the day melt away,
and fill your thoughts with love,
beneath a silent silver glow.

Trapper Boy

There isn't any time down here,
no seasons either, only darkness.

No clouds or blue sky, *not even the tip tapping of rain.*
When the carts come – *and they do come* – I open up
the heavy doors,

so I can't sleep-away this loneliness.
I'd like to run and jump,
or roll down a grassy bank until the world
becomes dizzy.

But my body has work to do,
so I drift away in my thoughts.
These dusty arms transform into wonderful

wings that unravel and stretch as wide as they like.
And how good it feels to stretch them,

to spread them and take flight,
to rise into sunlight.

(A 'trapper' was a term given to a child who worked in the tunnels of the underground mines, opening and closing the trap doors. Some started work when they were only four years old. It was a lonely, dangerous and dark place to be.)

Daydream

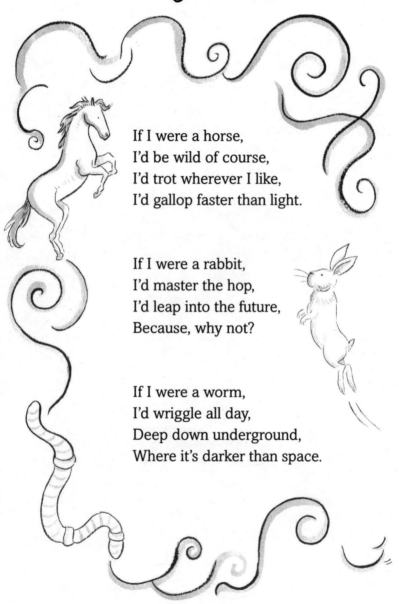

If I were a horse,
I'd be wild of course,
I'd trot wherever I like,
I'd gallop faster than light.

If I were a rabbit,
I'd master the hop,
I'd leap into the future,
Because, why not?

If I were a worm,
I'd wriggle all day,
Deep down underground,
Where it's darker than space.

If I were a tiger,
I'd rumble the day with my roar,
I'd swallow the sun,
And still be hungry for more.

But truthfully, I'm a child,
With no front teeth,
I'm addicted to cartoons!
And I dribble in my sleep.

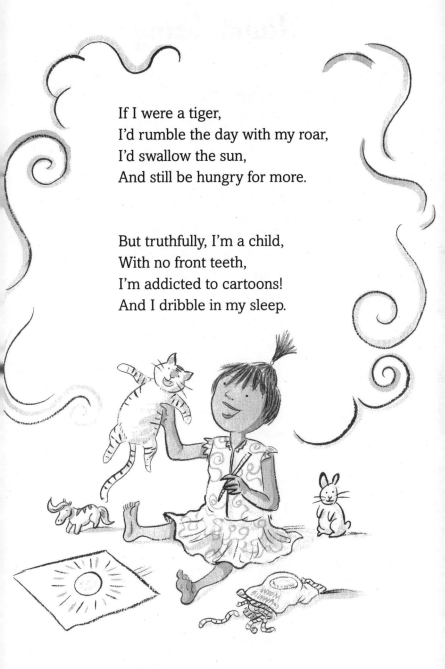

Quiet Things

When she leaves
home, her footsteps
are whispers upon

stone. When she pours
tea *nice and easy*,
it sings a quiet song

into the cup. And she
makes things with
ribbons and

bows, her hands
have the gentle
touch of

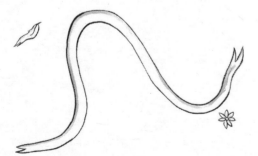

snow. And when
two clouds combine,
her thoughts are

tickled by the
glass-like chime.
And she sits

in peace,
drawing her
favourite quiet

things. Feathers,
bluebells and
butterfly wings.

Weeping Willow

I almost thought you
were sad,
until I saw you
as a slow
waterfall
of leaves,

almost still,

but closer every year
to saying *hello*,
to the gentle grass below.

A part of you peers
over the lake,
like a mother watching
her sleeping child,

and the lake holds its breath.

without a
single ripple to distort
your reflection.

If I could be any tree,
I would be you,
so calm, peaceful
and true.

Hector the Horrible Hedgehog

You think hedgehogs are cute?
Probably think hedgehogs are kind?
Well there lives one in my garden
and he's horrible most of the time,

Every night he trashes the place,
rocking and toppling my plant pots,
and laughing like a wicked witch,
he picks the locks to my shabby shed,
'I'm the king of the night!' he says.

He pees in my pond
and poops in the bird food.
the graffiti on my wall says:
EJOGS RULE!

He swipes the hat from my garden gnome,
shoots needles at my dog and steals his bone,
his terrifying teeth would be more suited on a bear,
I say I'm calling the police and he yells: *'Don't care!'*

We've tried to sell, but no one wants our home,
for as long as Hector the Horrible Hedgehog roams,
so we pick the poop from the bird food,
drain the pee from the pond,
and clear the broken pots away. Day after day.

EJOGS RULE!

Man in Town

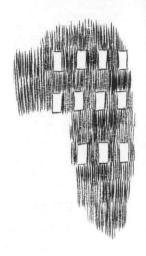

Who is that lonely
man in town,
curled up on the
concrete ground?

I see his breath
on winter's air,
but people pass
without a care.

His eyes are tired,
hands are worn,
clothes still damp
from the night before,

And I wonder if
dreams find him too,
underneath his
streetlight roof,

A dream to travel
from city streets,
out-of-sight,
to a safer sleep.

Who is that lonely
man in town,
curled up on the
concrete ground?

My Cloud

My cloud is my home,
with a smile all over its face,
floating around the world,
watching over the human race.

Sometimes we sail fast,
sometimes we sail slow,
at the beginning of each day,
the wind lets us know.

We rest beside the mountain,
sweep over secret seas,
if you saw my cloud float by,
you'd say it's the best you've ever seen!

Because my cloud is always smiling,
so I wear a smile too,
if every cloud has a silver lining,
mine is silver through and through.

Bubble Man

Froth is the bubble man's
worst enemy.
'Never shake the bucket,'
he says,
resting the bucket
on the ground
             (without a sound)
*'A bubble's emotion begins
in the potion.'*

He is quiet on his feet,
like a fox, and he only
ever wears purple clothing.
'Bubbles react better to purple,'
he says.
When he speaks, the occasional
bubble slips off his tongue.

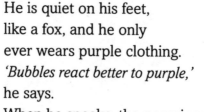

And there are faces on the
slick surface of each one.
All of them smiling and laughing as
they sail into sun shaped skies.
'Bubble shows what bubble knows,'
he says,
and when a bubble pops,
the laughter sprinkles over us.
Sweet as sugar, soft as snow.

Letter from a Football

Am I defined by this?
Defined by being kicked?
I see myself, as a moonless
leather planet in momentary orbit,
and it's true that in the end, like all
sublunary things, gravity finds me.
(I'm not the ball I used to be)
                    I'm less bouncy
but I still dream
of free kicks and penalties,
the wind on my weathered skin,
and the combination of voices, cheering!
But listen;
I'm ready for retirement,
you could hide me under the bed, or lose
me in the tightly-squeezed
branches of a nearby tree,
because I'm all kicked out,
it's not you,
it's me.

Guilty

Hands in the air!
Turn around slowly,
open your mouth,
you look guilty to me!

Apparently you ate a
dirty Jellybean off the floor,
and it was covered in hairs –
that's against the law!

Stay right where you are,
and I wouldn't get smug,
they all start this way,
(the full-time thugs)!

You're coming with me,
you can't be trusted,
the whole village knows,
and we're all disgusted!

Bed of the Sea

Nobody sinks like me,
gentle as a feather,
to the bottom of the ocean,
the bed of the sea,

Where fish of every colour
swim the depths of my sleep,
and plants are tickling
my toes.

Nobody bothers me,
not even the sharks,
it's a mystical world,
deeper than dark,

And when I'm ready,
I stretch my arms out wide,
then swim to the surface
of my sleepy eyes.

Lost Smile

Sometimes I just can't.
Not even by attaching the corners
of my mouth to my ear lobes
with bright yellow pegs.

Not even by hanging upside down
and allowing gravity to smile for me.
These stubborn cheeks still escape
looking happy.

I've tried forcing a smile and then
lodging my head in the freezer,
but all that freeze are my eyebrows,
like two frozen slugs.

My smile has gone away,
but I don't know where,
each day I wake up,
and still, it isn't there.

I just hope that it finds me,
so I can lose this disguise,
as pretend smiles don't hide
the sadness in my eyes.

Following Butterflies

Shhh ... it's over there,
approach slowly,
make your body small,
quiet your thoughts,
           (and off it floats again).

Aah, but not too far,
*a butterfly's hour is
measured in flowers.*
Careful though,
of the crunch and
crackles underfoot.

Now then, crouch again –
and slow your breathing,
if you can feel yourself moving
you're going too fast.

Look, just there,
blue wings are wide open,
cold blood, bathing in
midday's sun.

Enough warmth to
loosen the wing,
for weightless manoeuvring,
              (and off it floats again).

The Jam

Is so thick it wouldn't
flick off a stick.

The Jam

Is so sweet I had to
keep it discreet.

The Jam

Is so lovely, man!
It's out of hand, you understand?

The Jam

Is masterful,
each mouthful, a mini-miracle!

The Jam

Is running low,
oh no, don't go!

The Jam

Is looking empty,
it's a mystery, a tragedy!

Perhaps my neighbour will
make some more,
especially if I ask nicely.

Come By

Come by the owl,
come by the den,
but say hello to little wren,

See the silky meadow,
where the air is still,
and sunbeams are melting the hill,

Swoop by kingfisher,
take flight with kite,
then find a place for the night,

Somewhere near the lake,
where a red deer stood,
beneath the moon, beside the wood.

Solitary Bee

CALLING ALL BEES!
CALLING ALL BEES!
COME AND WORK LONG HOURS
FOR HER MAJESTY, THE QUEEN!

Sounds marvellous,
and awfully tempting,
but I'm a solitary bee,
I do my own thing!

I found my own nest,
and made it a home,
away from the chaos,
I'm happy alone!

My working day
is a gentle breeze,
I leave at ten,
I'm back by three,

And I might just fall
asleep on the job,
and that's ok,
because I'm the boss!

I do what I like,
is what I'm trying to say,
no orders or duties,
I do things my way.

So when you *call for all bees*
could you buzz off elsewhere?
Because I'm really quite busy
(washing my hair).

Caterpillar

```
            t  e
         a     r     i  l            r
This   c          p       l  a
```

has left lots of
little holes
in my apple tree leaves!

See, there's one
Look, there's three

'Yum Yum Yum on my Caterpillar tongue...
Munch Munch Munch on my favourite lunch!'

No way, I say,
Here, try this piece of cheese!
Even better, I say,
Try this custard cream!

```
            t  e
         a     r     i  l          r
But    c          p       l  a         please,
```

Stop eating all of my
apple tree leaves!

Star Keeper

He keeps stars,
some beneath the bed,
others on the dusty
tops of cupboards,
maybe one or two
in his old school shoes,
and when the darkest
night searches space
for light,
he gives them all away,
tiny presents
for the sky.

The Sea

What do you know
about the rhythm and flow,
and the deepening and
shallowing of the sea?

Are the waves still crashing,
and starlight still sparkling
on a surface our eyes
cannot see?

Are the sounds of water pooling
and looping and twirling,
only sounds if our ears
are near?

And does the belly of the ocean,
deeper black than the night,
still taste like the salt
of a tear?

Wonderful Words

I am a word
and I am with my friends,
together, we make
a sentence,
together, we write
poems and stories.
We are the skeleton
of song,
we live on page
and roll-off tongue.
Some of us not born yet,
Some of us covered in dust.
It's up to you,
to write, create, speak,
and sing us.
Good luck!

Maths Test

William goes for a picnic by himself, he takes…

3   Packets of crisps
4   Current buns
8   Chocolate digestives
2   Juicy plums
3   Mega bags of sweets
4   Cans of pop
1   Giant peach
8   Sticks of rock
1   Plate of spaghetti
3   Handfuls of grapes
1   Box of sticky toffee
1   Strawberry milkshake

How many items does William take?

Answer (Too many)

Midnight Wish

I'm a moon,
and I shine for you,

peeling through
winter's darkness,

borrowing light
from the sun,

and sprinkling it
on your roof.

I sweep shadows
from your eyes,

balance your ocean's tides

And this space, is all
that I know,

where I drift and glow

holding tight
to your midnight wish,

as I dip behind the hill,
and morning lifts.

The Teacher Said

Billy, stop being so silly!
Jane, stop playing in the pouring rain!
Michael, get off that motorcycle!
And Paul, stop growing so tall!

The teacher said,

Jim, don't say that to Tim!
Sabrina, don't do that to Christina!
Sally, give it back to Maggie!
Sorry. Maggie give it back to Sally!

The teacher said,

Jason, where's your concentration!
Kareem, snap out of that daydream!
Tom, stop keeping on!
Jay, turn around, walk away!

The children said,

Miss, what's this?
Sir, how'd you spell 'Errr'?
Mrs Gilbert, I'm stuck!
Mr Lee, when's dinner? I'm huuuuuungry!

Sometimes

I think about
breathing,
          my breathing.

and I change the
colour of the air,

violet, silver, gold –
it fills me,

          pooling in my stomach,
l e a p i n g   t o   m y   f i n g e r t i p s,

and rising like a tide
into my thoughts,

I'm a moon glow,
a silky sun,

and the world
is smiling.

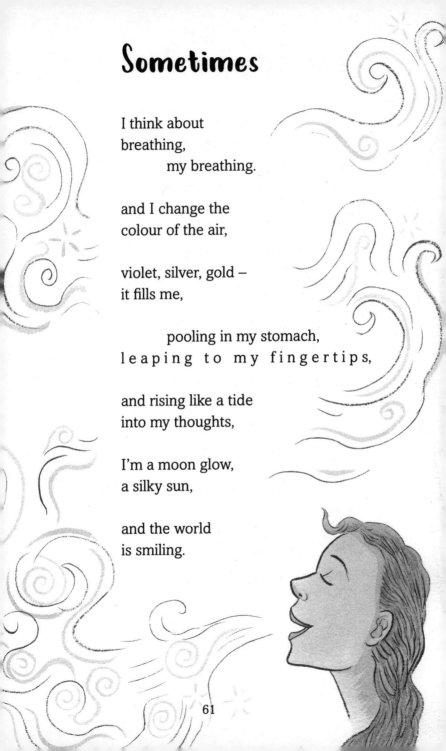

Acknowledgements

Here, I would like to thank:

Penny Thomas for recognising these poems and sharing my vision. Everyone at Firefly Press for their absolute brilliance, especially editor Leonie Lock who worked meticulously throughout. Philip Gross, for his wise and artful advice that has sharpened my tools as a poet, and a person. Katy Riddell, for adding life and magic to every poem. Della-Rose Hill-Katso, for her encouragement and Literature Wales for their continued support. All of my wonderful family and friends, every kind word has inspired me, for every way you have supported me, I am truly grateful and I thank you eternally. And to every pupil, teacher, head-teacher and parent/guardian – for all of your kindness and support, thank you.

Competition Winners

In September we ran a poetry competition which aimed to spark joy and imagination in 7-11 year olds. I'd like to introduce the magnificent competition winners: Sophie Macfarlane and Theo Janneh. I was thrilled to see how they crafted such wonderfully dreamy and imaginative poems, oozing with imagery, rhythm, and creativity. Wonder Thunder by Sophie has been crafted with pure joy and playfulness, and Underworld Dreams by Theo displays a depth of beautiful and vivid ideas that really tickle the reader's thoughts. Thank you both, and welcome to the book – you are published Poets!

Competition Winner

Wonder Thunder
by Sophie Macfarlane

Purple gorillas and neon yellow bats,
Killer robots and cheetahs wearing hats!
Boys wearing knickers and girls wearing trunks,
Vegan vampires and discoing monks!

96 year olds breakdancing,
And a zombie that's entrancing!
Cats that bark and dogs that meow,
Rainbow poo from an old smelly cow!

It's drawing to the end of this crazy rhyme,
WAIT! One more, bananas that tell the time!

Competition Winner

Underworld Dreams
by Theo Janneh

I see slimy, slippery, scaly fish
Not the type I'd like on my dish.
They are crimson red, like sunrise
With gills, frills, and robotic eyes.

I see vibrant, jagged, swaying coral
And fluorescent sharks looking floral.
The mischievous mermaids swish their tail
On curious cephalopod, they do sail.

I see giant starfish, as rough as golden sand
No brain, no blood, but are able to stand.
Wonderous whales tickle regenerated limbs
Like a floating rock, the Sea Star swims.